因為龍愛喝牛奶

Because Dragons Love Milk

By Marie Chow

Illustrated by Miki Tharp

They were halfway through dinner when Tycho announced,
"I don't want to go to bed tonight!"

當他們正在吃晚餐時, 阿慶突然說:
「我今晚不想睡覺。」

"Why not?" asked his
father.
爸爸問：「為什麼？」

"There are monsters under the bed!"
「我的床底下有怪物！」

"Monsters?" the father asked. "What kind of monsters?"
爸爸問：「怪物？什麼樣的怪物？」

2

Tycho was quiet for a while before saying,
    "A dragon. There's a dragon living under my bed."
阿慶想了一會兒，說：「龍。我的床底下有一條龍。」

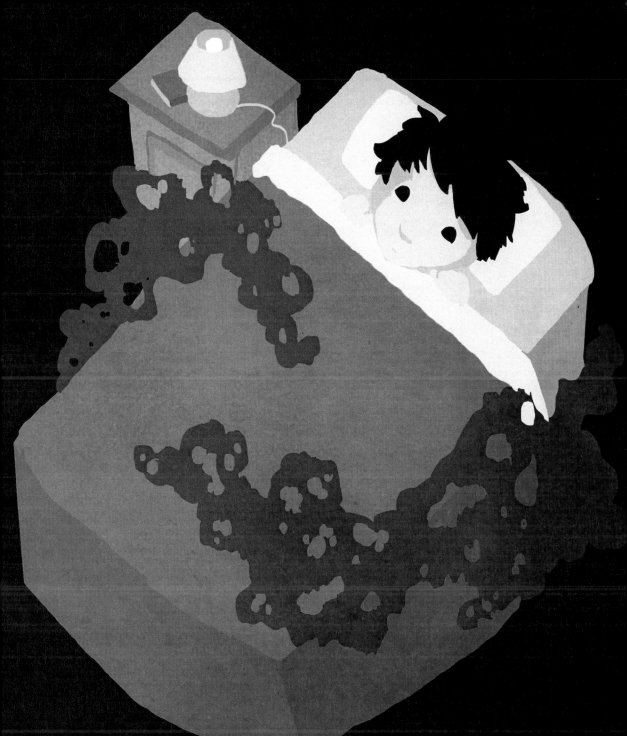

"A dragon?" the father repeated. "Well, no wonder you're having a hard time going to bed, she's probably huffing and puffing and keeping you awake with all that noise."

爸爸說：「龍？難怪你不能入睡。牠也許在不停的噴火，把你吵得不能睡。」

Tycho nodded his head vigorously.
  "Yes, yes, that's it exactly!
    What are we going to do about it?"
阿慶用力的點點頭說：
      「是的 是的 那我們該怎麼辦呢？」

"Well," the father said, "The thing about
dragons is that they love milk."

「是這樣的。」爸爸說：「龍其實很喜歡喝牛奶。」

"Milk?" Tycho repeated.
「喝牛奶?」

"Yes! You see, dragons' throats are almost always parched and dry from breathing fire.

「對了!就是這樣,因為龍不斷的噴火,所以牠會經常口乾舌燥。

The milk helps to soothe their sore throats."

而牛奶可以滋潤牠的喉嚨。」

"So this will make her happier?
        Because dragons love milk?"

「因為龍愛喝牛奶, 這樣會使牠舒服一點?」

The father nodded, "Exactly."

爸爸點頭説:「是的, 就是這樣!」

Tycho was halfway through his bath when he asked,
"But what about the alligator?"

阿慶在洗澡的時候, 突然問：「哪鱷魚呢？」

"The alligator?" the father asked. "You mean to
say you have an alligator under your bed as well?"
「鱷魚？你的床底下還有一條鱷魚啊？」

Tycho nodded. "And I have no idea what alligators like."

阿慶點了點頭：「可是我不知道鱷魚喜歡什麼」

The father thought for some time before saying,
爸爸想了一會兒，說：

"Well, I don't know if it will work for your alligator,
「我不知道你的鱷魚會不會喜歡喝牛奶，

but the one who lived in my closet was
partial to old shoes."
可是以前住在我壁櫥裡的鱷魚
喜歡啃舊的鞋子。」

14

"Shoes? Now you're telling me alligators like shoes?"

「鞋子？你的意思是鱷魚喜歡鞋子？」

"Oh yes. See, alligators are terrible about dental hygiene. They don't floss regularly, and so their gums are always hurting."

「是的。鱷魚平時不好好的清洗牠們的牙齒,也不用牙線，所以牠們常常會牙齦痛。」

"So chewing on a shoe makes their teeth hurt less?" Tycho asked.
「所以咀嚼鞋子會減輕牙痛？」

"Now you're getting it!"
「現在你開始明白了吧！」

16

The father was halfway through tucking Tycho into bed
when the little boy tugged on his sleeve and whispered,
"What about the T. rex?"
爸爸在給阿慶蓋毛毯時, 阿慶悄悄的問：
「哪暴龍呢？」

17

"Oh, you've seen her too?" the father asked,
reaching for the stack of books next to the boy's bed.
"Don't worry, I've got her covered."

「哦，你也看到牠了？」爸爸拿了一本書，然後說：
「不用擔心，我已經想到了一個解決辦法。」

"See, the T. rex --"
「其實暴龍...」
"Wait, wait, don't tell me: you're going to say
she likes being read to?"
「等一下，你是不是想告訴我牠喜歡聽故事？」

The father smiled, "Yes, because her arms are so short,
she can't hold the book open by herself."
爸爸笑了：「是的,
因為牠的胳膊太短, 所以牠不能自己打開書本。」

"So reading to her will lull her into sleep?"
「如果牠聽了故事，是不是會睡著呢？」
The father opened his book and said,
"You've got it."
爸爸翻開了書：「你答對了！」

As Tycho's eyes closed, he managed a faint whisper, "Can there be monsters again tomorrow night?"

阿慶閉著眼睛時，低聲問：「明天晚上這裡會不會再有怪物？」

The father smiled, "Of course."

爸爸笑著說：「當然會。」

Made in United States
North Haven, CT
18 October 2021